Stand Against Darkness

A Small Town Secrets Short Story
A.K. Hughey

Raven's Call Publishing

Contents

CHAPTER ONE

"No," Lee shouted, barely dodging a haymaker before sprinting down a trash-strewn alleyway between two dilapidated buildings. Taking the alley was risky, but the group had quickly surrounded him. Now, he didn't have a choice. Even if they had intentionally herded him toward the darkened route, he couldn't have resisted taking it; there were too many of them to fight.

"I'm gonna rip that purple hair off your scrawny head," a male voice yelled over the slapping of many shoes on asphalt as the group gave chase. Lee reached the end of the alley and panicked. At first, it looked like a dead-end, but there was a narrower alley to his right that led away between the buildings. He pushed off his toes, thankful he'd run track in high school, and beat feet toward the street light on the other end.

The night air was cold, and his frantic breath warmed his face as he desperately tried to escape. He'd been lucky before, evading the same group of teens over the past week, but tonight, they'd been strategic about cornering him.

Lee's focus had been on their shouting and hyena-like laughter behind him—and running for his life. He hadn't immediately registered the ankle sticking out at the edge of the building. It was too late when he finally realized a person was waiting just around the corner.

He slowed and ducked, but his attacker must have expected that because he tackled him low. They spilled to the sidewalk, Lee's right shoulder taking the brunt of the fall. He scrambled to his feet, but a hand caught his ankle before he could bolt again. Falling hard, he scraped his palms on the rough concrete. He looked over his shoulder and found a young man's twisted, wild face. The kid couldn't have been more than seventeen but was still built like a linebacker. Lee knew he would feel this fall in the morning–if he could get away this time.

"Hold up," a woman's strong voice broke through the sounds of the scuffle as the rest of the group emerged from the alleyway. Lee craned his neck to look up and found a petite, skinny woman leaning against the red brick exterior. She held a cigarette between the fingers of her right hand and had the other hand stuffed in the front pocket of her jeans. Her black hair was tied back, and her tawny brown skin glowed in the soft, amber light over the entrance to Ginger's, a small pub and grill he'd walked by at least a dozen times in the past two weeks.

Before he could say anything, rough hands dragged Lee backward and flipped him over, slamming his head on the pavement. His gaze found the evil smiles of the young men standing over him.

"Got your ass now," the apparent leader said with a grin, his dark eyes so obscured in shadow that Lee thought he looked like a demon.

"Stop it now!" the woman in front of the bar commanded.

No one listened.

Lee kicked out at the leader's knee, and the young man howled as he dropped to the ground. Turning, Lee scrambled away from the group, but many hands gripped his limbs and pulled him backward.

"Help!" Lee screamed, searching for the woman. He knew what was coming and hoped there would at least be a witness this time. His heart sank as she opened the door to Ginger's and disappeared inside. For a brief moment, he let his body relax as he surrendered to the wolves surrounding him and their insatiable bloodlust.

But before the bar's door closed fully, it opened again, swinging inward before the woman reemerged with a baseball bat in one hand.

"All right, you little shits," she growled the words loud enough for everyone to hear. "The cops are on their way. Better run back to your mamas." Everyone stopped, and even Lee was stunned at her nerve. The sudden projection of a thundering voice from the tiny woman in a white T-shirt and blue jeans would have surprised anyone.

She walked down the steps with her half-burned cigarette in her left hand and the bat in the other, pausing only ten feet from the cluster of bodies. Tension vibrated in the air around them.

"Go back to the kitchen," one man started to say as he walked toward her, "And make me a—"

The woman put her cigarette between her teeth and grinned as she gripped the bat with both hands and cocked it back. Stupid as he was, Lee didn't expect the young man to keep approaching her, but he did anyway, holding up his arm like a shield as she swung the bat with all her might.

There was a collective groan of shock as the bat connected with the man's arm and broke it instantly. Lee could barely hear the sickening crack above the shocked mutterings of the mob around him. A few hands let him go, but he was still too stunned to fight off those whose hands remained.

He watched in horror as two men rushed the woman together. She ducked the first and let him run past her as she slammed the end of her bat into the jaw of the second, dropping him to the ground to spit out a handful of broken teeth. She spun immediately, whirling the bat at the second man and grand-slamming it into his face before he could get close enough to swing on her.

The second man joined the first, lying on the sidewalk, groaning, crying, and bleeding. The woman grinned and twirled the bat with one hand while she cooly pulled her cigarette from her mouth and exhaled a cloud of smoke.

"Who's next?" she challenged, her bat slung ready over her shoulder. Before anyone else could step forward, sirens broke the night air and gradually grew louder. The hands still holding Lee finally released him, and he fell to the sidewalk, pain overwhelming his senses as the adrenaline wore off. He rose to his knees and cradled his aching right arm from when the big guy had tackled him. The mob worked together to carry their injured friends and disappeared in the opposite direction of the sires.

The wild-eyed leader was last to go. He stared out from the darkness, and Lee knew it wasn't over yet. They would be back and more blood-thirsty than ever–and now for the woman's blood, too.

She ducked into the doorway and tossed the bat inside before jogging to Lee. She knelt beside him, and he met her worried, deep brown eyes.

"Thank you," he said softly, fighting the lump rising in his throat. "I thought they were gonna..." He trailed off, unable to say the words out loud.

"I wasn't going to stand by and watch that go down, hon." She placed a gentle hand on his shoulder. "Are you okay?"

"I'm starting to feel it. My shoulder hit the ground pretty hard when they took me down, but I don't think anything is broken. I'm not losing blood, am I?"

She examined his head before replying. "You've got a good knot, but I don't see any active bleeding. Sit over here." As she helped him sit up against the wall of the bar, a pair of county cops in a marked car pulled up, turning off the siren as they parked along the curb.

"I'm Shelby. What's your name?" the woman asked, keeping her eyes on him even as the cops exited their car.

"Lee," he replied before turning his gaze from her to the cops.

CHAPTER TWO

"What's going on here?" a man with a deep voice asked, pulling her attention away from Lee. Shelby turned and looked up into the faces of two county cops. Given the bar's location on the outskirts of a small town with a nonexistent police department, the County Sheriff's Department usually responded faster than the state troopers. One of the two cops before her now was short, maybe five-foot-seven, and the other was easily over six feet. Being only a few inches over five feet herself, they practically towered over her, but she'd never been intimidated by anyone's size.

"A huge group attacked this kid—"

"Isn't this the same one we picked up last week?" the short cop interrupted Shelby, turning to face his partner.

"Yeah," the tall cop replied. His pale face was set with icy blue eyes, a sharp but moderate nose, and a strong jaw. He looked like the stereotypical high school quarterback, the prom king, the alpha jock who treated those around him like dirt. Shelby quickly decided she didn't like him. She studied his name tag as he mulled over the short cop's question: Sgt. Douglas.

Douglas's partner had distinct features: light olive skin, ebony black hair, and thick, black eyebrows overshadowing almond-shaped, sea-green eyes. His name tag read, 'Russo.'

"Lee Masaki?" Douglas asked.

"Yes, sir," Lee replied softly. Shelby turned to him, but he hadn't looked up to the cops, long locks of purple hair hanging over his face.

Douglas walked closer to Lee and knelt beside him, hands propped on his knees while his partner stood back. "What happened this time?"

"It's the same guys." Lee rubbed his shoulder. "They were waiting for me. They had a plan this time."

Shelby's stomach tightened as she watched the tears slide down the young man's cheeks. This young man was at the end of his rope, and she recognized his condition all too well because she had been there herself. Before she'd found her purpose, she had spent most of her life in this state. And some days, she still struggled.

"Could you identify them?"

"I know what they look like, but we didn't exactly stop to share phone numbers."

Douglas sighed, but he sounded more sympathetic than Shelby had expected.

"And where do you come in?" Russo demanded.

Shelby could barely restrain herself from an indignant eye-roll. She looked to Douglas first as he seemed to be the more senior of the two. He maintained a poker face as he rose to his feet again.

"I was on my break when I heard shouting. This kid came racing out of the alley, but one of the guys was waiting for him. He tackled Lee here, and started beating on him until the rest of the mob came outta that alley and joined in."

"And then what?" Douglas asked, resting his hands on his duty belt.

Shelby shrugged, her gaze drifting toward Lee. "I broke it up."

"Did you consider that maybe he," Russo pointed toward Lee, "might have done something to provoke these people?"

"I know this kid," Douglas interjected before Shelby could bite out something that would land her in jail for the night. "I'm pretty sure he didn't do anything wrong." He shot Russo a stern glance, and the junior officer didn't press the idea further. He turned his gaze back on Shelby. "How did you break it up?"

"First, I shouted at them, but they didn't stop. It looked like they were gonna kill him, so I ran inside and grabbed the first thing I could find."

"What was that?"

Shelby shrugged, shifting her weight. "A bat."

Douglas raised an eyebrow.

"Three came at me," she said without waiting for him to respond, "but I fought them off. The whole group ran off when they heard your sirens, officer."

"Deputy," he corrected smoothly before continuing. "So, you fought off three of these attackers by yourself?" Douglas looked her up and down, his skepticism apparent.

"She did," Lee said. "The first one threatened her and started after her, but she defended herself. Then two more rushed her together, and she dropped them both."

"Are you used to trouble, Miss?" Russo asked, his stance wide and his hard eyes boring into hers.

"Nope. But I like to be prepared."

"Okay, I'll need statements from you both." Douglas shook his head. "Lee, do you need to go to the hospital?"

They all turned to the young man and waited. Finally, he nodded. "It hurt like hell when I got tackled, and one of them slammed my head on the sidewalk, too. If there aren't four of you deputies standing there, I might have a concussion."

"All right. Give me a minute," Douglas said before pulling Russo back toward the car. He alternated between talking to Russo and speaking into the radio attached to his uniform. Russo shook his head vehemently and glared back at Shelby and Lee, and she knew the short man was more trouble than his pretty boy partner.

Douglas pointed a finger and growled low at Russo, but they were too far away for her to catch it. She did, however, hear Russo huff before stalking off down the alley Lee had emerged from earlier. Lee gave Douglas a statement, and Shelby excused herself to check in on the pub. Only two of her regulars had been inside when she stepped out for her break, and upon reentering, she found them both still staring bleary-eyed at the flatscreen over the bar.

"How's the game?" she asked, stepping behind the counter to refill their beers.

"Lost another bet," one man, Anthony, grumbled.

The other, Mike, grinned and nodded his head but said nothing, still glued to the action on the court.

"Well, then. This next round is on me."

That perked them up, but the pair cheered only half-heartedly as they watched their team falter in the third quarter.

"Need anything else? I have to step out again."

Anthony waved her away after he and Mike accepted their fresh half-pint glasses. This would be the one night she was thankful the pub was empty. She had left the bar unattended, but her boss, Ginger, knew both of the regulars, and she would understand and, more importantly, agree with Shelby's reasoning.

Douglas was still speaking with Lee when she stepped out into the frigid evening air again. A scowling Russo leaned against their cruiser. Fluffy, white snowflakes drifted from the sky, dancing in the gentle breeze as she returned to Lee.

"Can you give me your statement after we load him up?" Douglas asked as an ambulance arrived without fanfare and parked behind the cruiser.

"Of course," Shelby replied, glancing at Lee. She felt oddly responsible for the kid now, and she worried about his possible concussion. She watched as Douglas greeted the paramedics, speaking quietly and quickly. They nodded in response, and Shelby stood beside the cop to watch the paramedics strap Lee onto a stretcher and load him into the back of the ambulance. When they left toward the county hospital, Douglas turned his attention back to Shelby.

"You must be freezing," he said, and she watched him eye her bare arms.

She shrugged but didn't answer immediately. The air was frigid, but she was too stubborn to admit she was cold. "Do you mind coming inside? I'm not supposed to leave the bar unattended for this long. And to thank you, I'll start a fresh pot of coffee."

"Sure," Douglas agreed, gesturing in one hand toward the pub's entrance. Russo straightened, catching Shelby's eye, and she was instantly annoyed to know he'd join them.

Back inside, Mike and Anthony were still glued to the basketball game and had plenty of beer left in their glasses.

"Please, have a seat," Shelby offered hospitably before heading around the counter to start the promised coffee. Douglas sat first, and Russo followed his lead, looking increasingly disgruntled. Once the coffee started percolating, she leaned against the bar and met Douglas's gaze. "Where would you like me to start?"

"The beginning," Douglas replied, clicking his ballpoint pen.

She started immediately, describing in a straightforward manner how she'd been on her smoke break when the mob had chased Lee out of the alleyway. Careful not to incriminate herself, she kept the description of her involvement brief and to the point.

"Why would you do that for some stranger?" Russo blurted skeptically, his narrow eyes studying her.

"Wouldn't you? Isn't that what you signed up for?" Shelby retorted, glaring at him.

"Maybe, but it's my job. It's not your job to get involved–"

"Did you get a good look at these guys?" Douglas interrupted. It was a welcome relief to Shelby as tension filled the air between her and Russo. She knew better than to be on the wrong side of any cop, but she was also too hard-headed to back down when she should.

Turning her gaze back to Douglas, she shrugged. "I guess. They were all mid-to late-teens, mostly white kids, but a few others too. There were too many of them, and it all happened pretty fast. I think the one leading them had dark hair cut in a fade, long on top."

"Clothing?"

"T-shirts and jeans, nothing out of the ordinary." Shelby shrugged before turning and checking the coffee. "We have a security camera that points out front. It probably caught everything out there."

"Why didn't you mention it before?" Russo demanded.

"Russo, will you go out and canvass for more witnesses?" Douglas turned in his seat, squaring his shoulders at his partner.

"I already—"

"I think I saw a few bystanders. Go ask around."

"Fine," Russo grumbled.

"Here." Shelby poured coffee into a to-go cup and held it forward. "Fresh coffee?"

Russo glared at her as she held the cup over the bar. "I'll pass." He trudged out the door.

"Excuse him." Douglas sighed and shook his head slightly. "He's new."

"Never thought I'd see the day a cop turn down coffee," Shelby replied with a snicker. At least she had tried to offer peace in a cup and was now clear on where they stood. Douglas, on the other hand, held her gaze with gentle eyes and relaxed shoulders. There was something different in the air between her and this jock cop.

"I'll take it," Anthony piped up, giving her a much-needed respite from the growing silence as he reached across the counter.

"Great." She passed it to him before turning back to Douglas. "What about you? Will you turn down my coffee, too?"

He shook his head. "I'd love a cup of coffee, ma'am. Can you send us the recordings from the camera out front?"

"I'll have the owner send it. She's the only one who has access to the videos. All I can see are the live feeds." She pointed to a small monitor near the register. Three feeds split across the wide screen.

She turned and filled a ceramic mug as he surveyed the screen. When she turned back, she noticed a certain sparkle in his eyes.

"Have you known Lee long?" he asked before taking a sip.

"No, I hadn't met him before tonight. Although he does look vaguely familiar," she admitted and leaned against the bar.

"He's been hanging around here for about a month now. He's homeless, but he's a good kid. Aged out of the foster system a little over a year ago," Douglas explained. "We find a reason to bring in kids like him in the winter so at least they'll have a warm place to stay and get a few meals before we drop the charges."

"Why not take them to a shelter instead."

Douglas shook his head. "A lot of them don't want to go. Either the rules are too strict, the shelters are full, or they've had a bad experience and won't go back. Lee has a few precious items that he doesn't want stolen, so he keeps moving and sleeps on the street."

"That's awful," Shelby blurted before she could stop herself. "I mean, he doesn't have anywhere to go? No family?"

"None that he's mentioned to me."

"That's just tragic," she muttered, shaking her head before turning to pour herself a cup of coffee.

"His parents died when he was young, and he didn't have any other family to step up and take care of him. The older these foster kids get, the harder it is to find families to adopt them. Once they age out of the system, they're cast out into the world without much of a safety net. Many of them also lack any sort of trust that others will stick around and help them."

"So, what do you think happened tonight?" If she thought about Lee's dismal situation too much, she had to face that it could have been her out on the streets and in a similar position only a few years earlier.

Douglas scoffed and shook his head. "These damn kids have been chasing him all over town. He'll hide and lose them for a while, but they find him again. They just won't leave him alone. I swear they're gonna kill him if they get their hands on him again."

"What can be done? How do you stop that from happening?" she asked, incredulous at the idea these little monsters could get away with hunting Lee down and possibly beating him to death if they did catch him.

Shelby watched as Douglas's expression melted from the chiseled, formidable, stony face of a deputy at the height of his youth to a tired, soft-eyed man worn away by the demons clawing at his soul. Before she could fully register it, pity softened her hardened heart. If he was one of the good ones—and he seemed like he was—then the dark realities of his job were likely eating away at him.

"I can't do much until I catch them, and even then, it would be tough to get any charges to stick. I'm pretty sure I know the ringleader and his main crew, and if I'm right, their families have money. They'd be out quick on bail with minor charges and probably sue the county or the city, whoever happens to pick them up."

"So, what happens next?"

"I need to get Lee off the streets. He's vulnerable out there but refuses to go to the shelters. Like some others, he's had a few too many bad experiences."

"Bring him here," Shelby said before she could stop herself. It might be foolish since she didn't know the kid and what kind of trauma might color his attitude, mental health, and behavior. Maybe overconfidence drove her decision, but she was sure she could handle herself.

"What?" Douglas asked, even though she knew he'd heard her.

"I have a two-bedroom apartment upstairs," she explained, pointing toward the ceiling. "I don't want him getting killed by these little scumbags. How old is he?"

"Nineteen. Listen, you don't even—"

"Then he's old enough to work. He can work here, bussing and serving food if he wants. Ginger lets me hire and fire, so I'll take him on. He'll have a safe place to stay with me, access to a shower, a safe place to keep his things, and a decent job if he wants it. I'll even get him clothes if he needs them."

Douglas only stared for a moment, his blue eyes studying her intensely. She grinned, knowing he was questioning her intelligence and sanity.

"So you'll take in a homeless kid you just met tonight?"

"Damn straight." She lifted her coffee mug without breaking eye contact. "What do you think?"

Douglas didn't reply immediately. He looked around the bar, then back at her. "Your place is clean?"

"I keep my apartment as clean as I keep the bar. I haven't been using the spare bedroom.

"I mean 'clean' like–"

"Oh, yes. I don't drink or use drugs."

"Good." He nodded and sipped his coffee, looking away for the briefest moment.

"My place is pretty tiny, but it's better than the streets."

"You're right," he conceded before finishing his coffee. "I'll go to the hospital and pass your offer to Lee. If he agrees, I'll bring him back here tomorrow."

"I appreciate that, Deputy." Shelby couldn't stop a smile from warming her face as she stared at him. He seemed honestly concerned for Lee's welfare, and that compassion touched a hidden part of her heart. It reminded her that no one could be generalized too broadly based on things such as their appearance or the work they chose.

Grinning broadly, he nodded to her before standing. She fought to hold back the unwelcome warmth that threatened to brighten her face further.

CHAPTER THREE

S helby had heard nothing by noon the next day when she opened the pub. As she started the food orders for two women who had stopped for their lunch break, the pub's phone rang.

"Ginger's Pub and Grill," she answered, hoping she hadn't missed the call entirely.

"Miss Ford?" a man asked, and she instantly recognized Deputy Douglas's voice's smooth, low tenor.

"Hi, Deputy. How is Lee?" She walked back to the kitchen, pinching the phone between her shoulder and cheek so she could put on gloves before starting the food order.

"Great. I have Lee, and a few of the guys here at the department pitched in. We took him shopping for clothes, hygiene products, and a few more things. A reporter got wind, and they want to film an interview with Lee, you, and a few of our deputies." Shelby's stomach dropped, and her hands froze while chopping lettuce. "Can you be ready for the interview in an hour?"

She ripped off her food gloves and grabbed the receiver from her shoulder. "No. No, I can absolutely not."

There was a brief pause before he responded. "What? Why not?"

"I... I can't. I can't be on TV or have my name in the papers," she sputtered. She put a single trembling hand to her forehead. *I shouldn't have said that,* she thought, mentally kicking herself. There was a long silence, and she didn't try to fill it.

"Are you in trouble?"

"No, of course not," Shelby hurried to reply. It was mostly true, anyway. She had to think fast. All of her prior ideas about what she would do in this exact situation had somehow evacuated her mind. "I'm hiding."

"From what?" Douglas asked, his voice drenched in skepticism.

"Not a what, a who. An ex," she explained, lying outright this time. A cop would never understand her life and why she needed her anonymity. "He was controlling and abusive, and I barely got out with my life." That part was the one truth she could share with Douglas. Statistically speaking, she shouldn't even be alive after being taken by human traffickers.

"Oh," he finally replied, but she could still hear the doubt in his voice.

"I don't know if I'll make it if he finds me again," she whispered, fearful her voice would crack if she spoke any louder.

If her enemies saw her on TV, they would know where she worked and lived, and they'd learn her real name. She didn't want the trouble of finding a new place to hide again. If they found her, it would be harder to fall under the radar again.

"We were hoping this would help us get more donations for the county's homeless initiative—"

"I'll do anything I can to help, but I can't have my name out there or attached to the pub. I can't be on TV or in pictures," she reiterated. Then, another thought struck her mind. "What if I get Ginger? She's the owner, and since I'm her hiring manager, I'm merely acting on her behalf. This is really her generosity, not mine," she insisted.

"That's not the truth," he argued, but his voice had noticeably relaxed. "But if this is how it needs to be, then I understand. Please ask Ginger."

"I will. I'll have her here by the time you're ready."

"Great. We'll be there by one."

"Okay, bye."

Shelby hurriedly dialed Ginger and explained the situation. Thankfully, her boss was entirely on board with everything, including the interview for the news station. Thankfully, Shelby was doing more for Ginger than simply managing the pub; she and her friend Lucia were also helping search for Ginger's missing daughter. Their support had brought on Ginger as a friend and fierce ally to their cause, and she had expressed her willingness to do anything to help them.

The soft-hearted woman that she was, Lee's story had moved Ginger deeply, and Shelby had known it would. As long as the kid wanted it, he would have a home with them, and Ginger would mother him whether he liked it or not.

CHAPTER FOUR

O n Ginger's advice, Shelby spent the interview time at the gym, getting in some cardio before lifting weights and then enjoying the steam room. Even as she made the most of her workout, her mind was busy overthinking her misstep with Deputy Douglas. Ginger assured her all would be well, and she would stick to the script if anyone asked about Shelby, but the situation still unnerved her. Hopefully, after Lee moved in, she wouldn't have to see Douglas or his colleagues again and endure further questioning.

When Ginger texted her with the all-clear, Shelby returned to the pub to find Lee sitting at the counter. Ginger leaned over it from the other side, deep in conversation with him. Her long, curly red hair hung loose over her shoulders, and she wore a frilly, forest-green blouse. The gritty but sweet woman's love for her near-pure Irish heritage was second only to her love for her children.

Shelby was glad to see Lee had a new haircut and wore clean new clothes and winter boots. She noticed his eyes looked brighter as he turned to greet her.

"Shelby!" He jumped out of his seat to meet her, and she hesitated. She wasn't usually a huggy person, but something about this kid unearthed her softer spots. Opening her arms, she welcomed him into as warm an embrace as she could manage. Ginger smiled and nodded from the bar, a glimmer of tears in her green eyes.

"Come on," Shelby said softly. "Let's have lunch."

When Lee pulled away, she spotted tears rolling down his cheeks. "I'm sorry," he muttered, wiping them away with trembling fingers. "Nobody's hugged me in over a year. And it feels strange to have people listen when I talk instead of pretending not to hear me, instead of flinching away and looking grossed out when I want to shake hands." He broke down into sobs, and Shelby fought the wave of emotion threatening to rise inside her. She was harder than this; why was she suddenly ready to cry with this young man?

"Douglas said he'll be back later," Ginger said with a wink as Shelby gestured for Lee to retake his seat at the bar.

Shelby tried to pretend she hadn't seen the wink. "Why?"

"To check on everyone, I suppose." The older woman shrugged and picked up a steaming mug.

"What's the tea today?" Shelby asked as she walked toward the kitchen.

"Breakfast in Paris," Ginger replied excitedly. "It's delicious."

"I swear you have a new favorite every day." Shelby laughed as she headed into the kitchen.

After quickly preparing a grilled chicken salad, she rejoined Lee and Ginger at the bar. "So, you're all moved in upstairs?" she asked before taking her first bite.

He nodded, his mouth full of Ginger's famous goulash. Despite her obsession with the Irish part of her heritage, she loved all kinds of food, especially the Polish-American comfort foods popular in the region.

"The bed is nice," he observed before shoving another spoonful of goulash into his mouth. "I... I love it. Thank you."

"Thank Ginger," Shelby corrected.

"Yeah, right. Don't let her fool you," Ginger warned Lee. "She's hard on the outside but a big softie inside."

Lee laughed, and Shelby didn't bother arguing with her boss and friend. "Did you decide if you'd like to work here?"

He nodded. "Ginger said I can buss and clean. If you'll train me, I'd also like to work in the kitchen."

"You would?"

"Yeah," he said with a laugh. "I love cooking. Besides, she said you need a hand with that."

Shelby raised an eyebrow at Ginger, who was barely containing her laughter.

"Anything you're willing to take on, we'll let you do. Except serve alcohol, of course," Ginger added.

Lee's face softened, and he looked like he would cry again. Shelby reached out and laid her hand on his.

"It's okay," she said gently, hoping to comfort him.

"Nobody gave me a chance for years," he choked. "Why do you want to help me?"

"Because it's the right thing to do," Shelby replied easily. "Ginger and I," she said, looking up at her boss, whose face was also streaked with tears, "we take care of people."

Ginger came around the corner to pull Lee and Shelby in a motherly hug. "That's right," she agreed. "You're safe now, kiddo."

CHAPTER FIVE

The following day, Shelby helped Lee complete his new hire paper-work. Thankfully, he had memorized his social security number, and the deputies had already helped him set an appointment with the Secretary of State to get a proper ID. She spent the late morning hours teaching him the menu and building a system for his first full day of training and work. Ginger had tried to get him to work only a few hours a week at first—rather than jumping straight in—but he had argued for more hours, insisting he was tired of being alone with his thoughts and nothing else to do after years of drifting on his own.

Shelby settled Lee in the kitchen before heading out front to unlock the door. Stepping outside for a pre-lunch-rush smoke, she was shocked to find no fewer than ten uniformed deputies standing in a gaggle near the door. Douglas stepped forward with a bright smile before she could say anything. Russo stood behind him, but he wasn't smiling.

"Can you handle a big party for lunch?" Douglas asked. "I even brought my boss." He pointed to a tall, muscular man who tipped his cap at her.

"Oh, yes. Absolutely. How much time do you have?" she managed to ask despite her surprise.

"About an hour."

"Head in and get settled," she said, running the menu through her head. "Your best bet is salads, subs, or burgers," she explained as she led the officers inside. They took seats as she got her checkpad and began taking their orders. "Are you responsible for all this?" she asked Douglas before taking his boss's order first.

"Of course!" He shrugged, and his colleagues chuckled. She smiled and tried to relax, thankful for the business, but she still worried that he would try to ask too many questions if she let him.

She moved quickly, turning in each table's order to the kitchen before getting coffee, water, and sodas out to their new customers. Once she had served all their drinks, she returned to the kitchen and directed Lee on building plates while she cooked the chicken and beef. After she finished the first set of orders, they began moving like a well-oiled machine, working together as if they'd done this a thousand times. As much as she had worried when all the officers had shown up unexpectedly, she was relieved when Lee proved a quick study.

"Have you worked in a kitchen before?" she asked, taking out two platters.

"Three," he replied, taking over the meat so she could deliver the finished plates.

"Damn," she muttered as she carried a platter in each hand. That was two more than she had worked in.

Within twenty-five minutes, they served all the deputies, and Lee began helping Shelby with drink refills. She heard a glass break behind her as she reached the Sheriff's table to see if they needed more refills.

Turning, she watched Russo jump out of his chair, sending it flying backward. "You clumsy little f—"

"Russo!" Sheriff Clarke roared, interrupting his subordinate before the man could finish what was probably a slur. Clarke rose slowly from his seat, and his inner circle seated around him followed his lead. He towered over them, and Shelby briefly wondered why the man hadn't chosen to be a professional wrestler instead of a cop. "Outside now!"

Russo's face reddened instantly, and he grabbed his cap before heading to the door.

"Excuse us, ma'am," Clarke said, nodding slightly before turning behind Russo and grabbing a handful of the man's uniform. He pushed his subordinate outside while the inner circle followed him. Douglas trailed them; anger had hardened his features. She watched as he walked by but didn't turn to meet her gaze.

"Are you okay?" she asked Lee as she approached the table where he stood frozen, his mouth hanging open. He gathered himself and nodded his head, but his hands trembled and his eyes were glassy. Shards of broken glass were scattered across the dark wood floor. "It's okay."

"Ignore that... guy," another cop said, shaking his head in disgust. "He's new."

"I don't think he's going to be here much longer," the deputy next to him observed before taking a bite of his burger.

"Lee, the broom and dustpan are—"

"I know," he cut her off as he turned away.

"Does anyone else need anything right now?" she asked the remaining half-dozen deputies who hadn't followed their Sheriff out.

"We're good," a few replied, and the others nodded.

Shelby hurried behind the bar to pour herself a shot of whiskey, slamming it before turning her attention to the feed from the security camera pointed out front. She watched in awe as Clarke hovered over Russo. They would have been nose to nose if Russo was anywhere near as tall as his boss. In a flash, the Sheriff's arm shot up and pointed down the street. Russo paused briefly before turning and marching away.

She wished she could hear what Clarke said to Douglas and the others after Russo disappeared from the screen. To her surprise and relief, it seemed that perhaps Russo was more of the exception than the rule—at least in this county.

If the Sheriff required discipline, respect, and good conduct of his deputies, Shelby would consider herself lucky to be within his jurisdiction. This small, rural town had about 1,500 residents, and their former tiny police department had closed years ago. Around here, the Sheriff's department or the State Troopers responded to calls.

When the Sheriff returned with his inner circle, they resumed their seats and continued their lunch. He nodded solemnly at Shelby, and she returned it with a grateful smile. Lee had disappeared into the kitchen, so she went to find him.

"Hey," she said as she rounded the corner. Lee scrubbed the food prep surfaces, his focus and determination clear. "Are you okay?"

"I hate when people call me that."

"Call you what?"

"Th-the... f-word," he mumbled.

"It's deplorable," she agreed. "He's obviously compensating." Her attempt to make him laugh failed, and Lee remained wrapped in his thoughts as he cleaned the kitchen.

"There's more, isn't there?"

"You do what you have to do out on the streets," Lee said through gritted teeth. "I did what I had to survive. That's why those assholes were chasing me."

"I don't understand."

"The leader, Jared, his big brother... He was drunk, and he blames that night on the alcohol, but he told his shithead kid brother." His busy hands stopped, and he pressed his hands on the counter, squeezing his eyes shut. "Jared's been out for my blood ever since he found out."

Shelby moved a step closer, nodding slowly. "I'm so sorry, Lee. I'm sorry for what you've had to go through, what you had to do. Now, you don't have to do that anymore. I mean, if you don't want to. Okay?"

"I don't," he sputtered, his voice trembling. "I'm so damn tired of being scared for my life."

"You're safe here," she reminded him, and she meant it with every fiber of her being.

CHAPTER SIX

Two weeks later, Shelby was serving Lee's newest menu item—spicy pineapple chicken wings—to a pair of deputies when Douglas called her.

"Hello, DD," she answered, calling him by the new nickname she had devised after seeing him almost every day for the past week.

"I hate that. Please call me Matt."

"Nah. That's not as fun, Deputy."

"Isn't there some other ridiculous nickname you can come up with?"

"Nope," she said, grinning as she refilled a customer's drink. "What can I do for you?"

"We want to throw a surprise party for the Sheriff, and I hoped–if it's okay with you–we could have it at Ginger's."

"When?"

"Thursday night. There will be about two dozen of us attending."

"We can handle that," she confirmed. "Thursday isn't usually a busy night for us, so we'll set it up and reserve an area for you."

"Will you be there?" he asked, catching her off-guard.

"Of course," she replied. "Anything special we need to do?"

"No, I'll come early and bring a few decorations. It'll be relaxed. We're pretty laid back."

Shelby tried and failed to stifle a chuckle.

"Is something funny?"

"I never imagined a group of cops to be relaxed and laid back."

"I'll bet we'll surprise you," he said, and she could almost hear his smile.

"Looking forward to it." Shelby was thankful he could be a good sport. "All right. We'll see you tomorrow night."

"Thanks, Shelby."

"Bye, DD," she said, eliciting a snort from the deputy.

Time flew as Shelby prepared for the party after talking it over with Ginger. After a week of increasing and unexpected visits by local law enforcement for lunch and dinner, Matt finally let her in on the reason: they wanted to patronize more businesses involved in uplifting the community. Their visits helped raise the pub to a profit after a particularly slow month. Shelby always had reservations after a few tense run-ins with the police, but none of those officers had seemed very kind or compassionate.

But over the past two weeks, she'd seen a different cop every day, and every single interaction had been uneventful, normal, and even pleasant.

Well, except any day when Russo appeared. He fit every nasty stereotype, and she was grateful she hadn't seen him again since the group of deputies had come for lunch after the news interview. She could only hope he would be on duty and unable to attend the Sheriff's party.

At five pm on Thursday, Matt was the first to walk in, a mix of male and female officers following close behind. After waving hello to Shelby, he immediately directed them to set up the decorations and push the tables together. Tonight, Ginger would manage the bar and help Shelby take orders and serve food for the fifteen or so officers, many of whom would bring their significant others. Matt, she observed, was one of the few who had not brought a personal companion. The preparations were complete within an hour, and everyone but the Sheriff had arrived. When he finally walked through the door, the group shouted, "Happy Birthday!" and Shelby, Lee, and Ginger joined in.

Clarke seemed surprised, but he only grinned and shook his head as his family came in behind him. Nothing should have surprised Shelby, but she did a double-take when the woman holding the Sheriff's hand walked in behind him. Her rich, ebony skin contrasted his pale features. Dropping her long winter coat from her shoulders, she revealed a heather gray sweater dress and dark gray knee-high boots. Three young adults walked in after Clarke's wife, and Shelby guessed they were the couple's older children. They looked more like Shelby with tawny light-brown skin. The sight of the family made her wonder what her own parents had looked like together.

When Sheriff Clarke sat at the head of the table with his family and friends surrounding him, Shelby strode over with her guest checkpad.

"Happy Birthday, Sheriff," she greeted him and his guests with a smile. "What would you like for dinner tonight?"

He looked up from the menu and smiled at her. "Thanks, Shelby. I'd like a glass of your best bourbon and the herb butter steak, medium rare, with mashed potatoes and..." He glanced at his wife. "A house salad."

She grinned and winked at him before turning her attention to Shelby. "I'll have a cabernet and the grilled chicken Caesar salad."

Going around the table, Shelby took all the orders and brought them back to Lee in the kitchen before helping Ginger prepare and serve all the drinks. As they served everyone's beverages, she inwardly groaned as she noticed Russo. She overheard him ask about the Sheriff's wife.

"They met at Ann Arbor," Matt explained. He smiled up at Shelby when he set his drink on the table. "She was pre-med, and he was studying criminal justice. Clara's an ER surgeon at the hospital in Saginaw."

"Wow," Russo replied, shaking his head. His mouth twisted downward, and he glared down the table. Shelby tried to brush off his venomous atmosphere as she moved out of earshot and finished serving the table.

Afterward, she assisted Lee in delivering the appetizers in record time, then worked with him on the dinner orders for the Sheriff and his family first. They went out quickly and managed to serve the entire table before anyone could ask for a second refill on their drinks. Considering the size of the party compared to the three-person staff, Shelby was proud of their work and timing. She stood at the bar and watched, waiting to refill drinks.

Matt rose from his seat and approached her as the Sheriff and his family finished their dinners. "It's time for the cake," he whispered, leaning in close. The faint scent of his cologne intrigued her, and she felt herself being drawn in against her will.

"Any special instructions?"

"Can I help?"

"Sure," she agreed with a shrug, keeping her poker face on.

They went to the kitchen, and Shelby pulled the cake from the fridge. It was already on a stand, and Matt quickly poked numbered candles into the frosting and lit them.

Ginger poked her head around the doorway. "Are we ready?"

"Yep," Matt replied, lifting the cake by its stand. He led them out of the kitchen, and they sang the birthday song together. The rest of the party quickly joined in singing. The Sheriff's face reddened, but an uncontainable smile broke through his stoic visage.

"I can't say enough to thank everyone for this," the Sheriff started after the cake was set before him and the singing faded. "You all are part of my family, and I trust that my family is part of yours. I couldn't ask for a better group of men and women to help me serve this county. Here's to another year of giving my best to our community." He toasted, raising his bourbon glass.

The table applauded his simple but sincere words and raised their glasses with him. They enjoyed their drinks–though not all imbibed–and went around the table so each member of the Sheriff's department could offer birthday wishes to their boss.

After finishing, the party loosened up a little, and someone started the jukebox. Ginger refilled drinks and helped pass out cake while Lee and Shelby cleared dinner plates. Remembering Russo's previous interactions with Lee, Shelby took the irritable cop's side of the long table as they bussed and cleaned up.

"Are you finished?" she asked Russo as she approached.

"Yes," he grumbled without looking up from his phone as he texted furiously. Her curiosity got the better of her, and she couldn't help but glance at his screen.

You better come before they all leave. Bring the boys.

She tried her best to ignore it, but worry settled in her stomach. Maybe more deputies would drop by later to wish their boss a happy birthday. Trying to shake it off, she moved down the table away from him. Russo's tension and venom had permeated the very air around him.

Once all the dinner plates were cleared and everyone had a piece of cake, Lee started washing dishes in the back while Shelby helped Ginger verify all the checks in the POS system. A bunch of the guys had pooled their money to cover the bill, and Matt had taken charge of making sure it got paid.

As she started around the counter to bring the check to him, the front door swung open. Six stone-faced men strode inside quickly and quietly, followed by four young men, all of whom Shelby immediately recognized. One had a sling on his arm, another's chin was green and yellow, the third was the one who tackled Lee, and the last was limping. She guessed his ribs still hurt even after two weeks.

"No good deed goes unpunished," she muttered as she set the check holder on the counter.

Matt must have heard her because he looked up then. "What?"

But she didn't have time to answer him. "Are you gentlemen here for dinner?"

"Sheriff," the man in the lead began, blatantly ignoring her. His blue eyes narrowed, glaring daggers at her before turning on Clarke. "I demand you arrest this woman immediately."

All conversation in the pub ceased, and the only sound left was the clatter of dishes being washed in the kitchen. Someone had even lowered the sound on the jukebox. Shelby hoped that Lee wouldn't get curious and wander out of the kitchen.

"Did you hear me?" he asked. He was tall, but he wasn't nearly as tall as Clarke, who dropped his napkin on the table as he stood.

"I heard you, Paul. What's this all about?" Clarke asked, sighing like this wasn't the first complaint he'd fielded from the man.

"This psychopath attacked my son and his friends," he spat, pointing a finger at Shelby.

She crossed her arms over her chest but remained silent, her veins throbbing as her heart beat faster. Surrounded by cops, she'd have no chance to escape if they wanted to arrest her. And the men who'd just arrived with accusations against her seemed to know the Sheriff. Last she heard, the county had no interest in prosecuting her for defending another person and herself against the reasonable threat of harm from others. They had already decided it was self-defense, but she now worried that if the kids' parents had some power and influence in the area, the county might be persuaded to reconsider prosecuting her.

Clarke pulled his phone from his pocket, tapped his screen a few times, and then showed it to Paul. The man's stoic face paled slightly before turning a deep shade of red, his chest heaving with angered breath.

"We couldn't identify the attackers until tonight," Clarke explained. He flashed the video on his screen to the room. "On behalf of the county prosecutor, we would like to thank you for your help in identifying the young men who pursued and attacked the teen in the video. Are you going to bring your sons in on your own, or do I have to arrest them in front of everyone here?"

"What about her?" Another father asked, pointing at Shelby. She watched him seethe with anger and denial.

Clarke shook his head. "Davis refuses to charge her. It was clearly self-defense, and we have bigger problems. In fact, she's receiving a citizens' award for protecting that young man from being beaten to death by your out-of-control kids." He turned back to Paul. "That free ride to Michigan? You can kiss it goodbye once Mason is sentenced. Now, I'm only going to ask nicely one more time. Are you bringing them in, or are we—"

"Sir, this woman is a criminal, and that kid is a homo," Russo interjected, standing up and striding over to face the Sheriff.

"What in the hell is wrong with you?" Clarke growled, his fists curling at his sides.

"And I know she's hiding some—"

"She is a hero," Clarke cut him off sharply. "And let's be clear on something very important: Mr. Masaki's sexuality isn't any of your concern. It does not assume his involvement in criminal activity or anything else the law is concerned with." He paused for a moment, then shook his head and added, "I knew I shouldn't have hired you. You are not fit to wear our uniform."

Russo trembled with fury as he looked up at his boss, and everyone in the room sat frozen in stunned silence. Shelby glanced at Matt. Without a sound, he had risen from his seat and quietly positioned himself beside her while the Sheriff had been speaking. His stance was hips-width, and he had crossed his arms over his chest, making his t-shirt hug his muscular biceps and shoulders. It was the first time she had seen his bright blue eyes so cold and fierce.

"But she hurt—" Paul started again.

"She not only saved Mr. Masaki from a vicious and likely fatal attack, but she also saved your boys from murder charges. You better thank her, Paul, because I'm not the one. None of us are." He gestured to his deputies. "We aren't the ones to be quiet, to abide by violence and hatred, whether it comes from the poor or the rich. We don't protect the few; we protect them all. We stand with Shelby and Lee, with Ginger," he declared, pointing at each of them. "We stand together against your hatred, against your delusional sense of superiority and your toxic nepotism."

Shelby felt her pride swell and her fear dissipate. For a brief moment, she didn't feel like it was just her against the world anymore. She looked around at the LEOs and their families, who had risen from their seats and now stood shoulder to shoulder. They represented a small army of people who looked up to a leader with integrity and a greater social consciousness. The feeling of community overwhelmed her.

"We'll meet you there," Paul said, his bravado failing. He clamped a hand on his son's shoulder and herded his small group out the front door. "We'll have our lawyers."

"That is your protected right," Clarke replied with a smile as he watched them go.

"Sheriff, you're wrong here. These people are crim–" Russo objected.

"No, *you* are wrong, Russo! Get your ass outta here and turn in your equipment immediately!" Clarke's bass voice vibrated through the room.

"Disgusting," Russo growled, his face and ears beet red as he stormed toward the door behind the local men and their sons.

After the last of the group exited and the door swung closed, Shelby tried to control the anxious trembling in her body and turned to Matt. He put a strong, warm hand on her shoulder. "Are you all right?"

She nodded. "I'm fine. I just...I never expected it would go this way."

"Clarke is a force to be reckoned with. And Russo is done for. He had a record, some issues with abuse of power and racial profiling. He swore up and down it was a witch hunt, and he wasn't like that. After he begged for a second chance, Clarke took him on. After all this, we'll make sure he's never in uniform again."

"You... you all protected me?" Lee's shaking voice called from behind them. Shelby turned around to find Lee, his purple hair covered with a bandana from working in the kitchen, and his face covered in tears.

"We did," Matt confirmed.

"And we will continue to do so." Clarke agreed as he walked through the group and held out his hand.

Lee accepted, and the big Sheriff shook his hand firmly before turning to Shelby and Matt. He smiled broadly and clapped a hand on each of their shoulders, then returned to sit beside his wife. After kissing her gently, Shelby could have sworn Clarke sent a mischievous nod at Matt.

READ MORE

In chronological order:

- Desecrate the Darkness - Book 1

- Walking in Darkness - Standalone short story available on Amazon.

- Stand Against Darkness - Standalone short story.

  - Would you like to read it for FREE? Head to www.akhughey.com/freestand

- Hunting Darkness - Short story originally featured in the Make Them Pay thriller anthology.

  - Would you like to read it for FREE? Head to www.akhughey.com/freehunt

- Together Against Darkness - Short story featured in the March For Justice anthology.

- Falling Into Darkness - Book 2

- Rising From Darkness - Book 3

Would you like updates about upcoming releases, live events, giveaways, and reader parties?

- Join my Dark Angels Reader Bulletin at akhughey.com.

- Get access to Bonus Content like flash fiction, more short stories, books, audio, and more when you join me on Ream: https://reamstories.com/shadowsandscreams

Acknowledgements

I would like to thank the members of the Author Transformation Alliance for actively providing feedback and support; Julie Wild for beta reading; Nan Sampson for editing; Mary B. Knapp for being my publishing inspiration and support throughout my writing journey; K. McCoy for sensitivity reading and for being my accountability partner; Emily Burch Harris for proofreading; Shawn Smith for pressuring me to write faster; and my parents, for encouraging me and instilling within me the belief that I could do anything.

I must also express my endless gratitude for my incredible cover designer, Kristen of Kristen Lee Design. Visit her at kristenlee.co.uk.

About the Author

Writing became A.K.'s passion from a young age, her notebooks quickly filling with high fantasy and science fiction short stories. What began as fiction writing evolved to consist mostly of report writing and formal business communication during her fourteen years of active and reserve duty in the United States Army. While pursuing her Bachelor of Arts in English with a concentration in Writing, she began contributing regularly to non-fiction magazines and first saw her byline in print in July of 2015.

After attaining her B.A. in English (Writing) and completing her M.A. in Ancient and Classical History, she has returned her focus to completing her many writing projects.

Connect with A.K. Hughey

Website: www.akhughey.com
Ream: https://reamstories.com/shadowsandscreams
Facebook: www.facebook.com/audreyiswriting
Instagram: www.instagram.com/audreyiswriting
Twitter: www.twitter.com/audreyiswriting
TikTok: www.tiktok.com/@audreyiswriting